Henry Seamouse

BY

Sam McBratney

illustrated by

Philippe Dupasquier

— LONGMAN —

The Cat and the Drum

The dusty old drum had been hanging from a nail in the garage for many years. No one paid much attention to it except Skinny Whiskers the cat, who often sat very still for a long, long time, looking up at it. She knew that Henry Seamouse and his seamouse friends lived in there.

3

Those mice had wild parties inside the drum. They sang songs about the sea and then they came outside and threw down peanut shells, shouting, "Yoo-hoo, Skinny Whiskers, it's raining peanut shells!"

"Just you wait, Henry Seamouse," the cat said to
herself. "One of these days I'll get you. I will juggle you
between my paws for ages and ages – and then ... then
I'll eat you!"

A Mouse with no House

Henry Seamouse was a fine looking mouse. His glossy coat never seemed dull or shabby, nor did he allow his large mouse ears to become clogged up with mud. His tail was rather short, for a ship's cook had once chopped off the end with a carving knife, but a little thing like that didn't worry Henry Seamouse.

What did worry him, though, was the day he came home from sea to find that his house was missing. The nail was still there, the string was still there, but ... no drum.

"It's gone," said Henry. "All of a sudden I'm a mouse without a house."

"Now what are we going to do?" said Mac, who was a bit grumpy. "If we have to sleep under flowerpots we'll all be eaten by that horrible cat. This is serious!"

But where had it gone? How could someone steal a whole house?

"We'll ask Blanche," said Henry. "She'll know what happened."

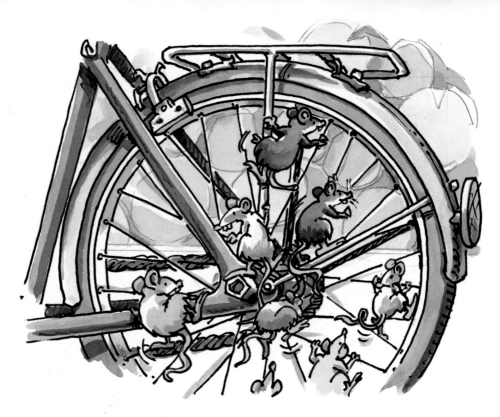

So Henry Seamouse and his seamouse friends climbed
through the spokes of a bicycle until they came to a
dark hole. Blanche knew Henry's knock and ran out
with her whiskers twitching.

"Oh Henry," she said. "I'm so glad you're back! Do you
remember that girl Emily Robinson who chased you
round and round the garden with a yard brush? She
took your house away. She's got it with her in there
where the cat lives. You'll never get it now, Henry – your
lovely house is gone forever."

"I think not," said Henry as he jumped up on the saddle of the bicycle. "Follow me, you mice. I may be a mouse without a house – but not for long!"

Emily Wants to Play the Drum

It was Emily Robinson's fault that Henry had no house. Emily was one of those people who always get what they want because they scream blue murder if anyone says NO to them. She was always saying "I WANT THIS!" and "I WANT THAT!" Emily didn't wait until Christmas for a new bicycle – she screamed blue murder until she got one in July.

One day she said, "I want to play the drum in the
garage."
"A drum is a very noisy thing, Emily dear," said her dad.
"I like noise," said Emily.
"But it's old and dirty and as dusty as could be,"
said her mum.

"Well clean it then!" yelled Emily, stamping her foot.
"I want to play the drum today and I won't wait until
tomorrow!"
So Emily's mum and dad cleaned up the drum and
brought it into the living room. They didn't know that

the famous Henry Seamouse lived in there.
But Skinny Whiskers knew. 'Just you wait, Henry
Seamouse,' she was thinking. 'You'll come for that
drum. This time you won't get away from me and I'll
have you for breakfast!'

Quick-March up the Roof

Twenty-four mice marched up the drainpipe; and when they came out of the drainpipe, they marched some more to the chimney pot right on top of the roof. Julia Sparrow was sitting there. "Henry Seamouse!" she cried. "What are you doing up here? Don't you know this is the roof?" She had never seen mice so high up in all her life.

"They took my drum," said Henry. "I'm a mouse without
a house, but I'm going to get it back again and this
chimney is the only way in."
He gave his whiskers a twirl and then he jumped into
the chimney pot, followed by all his seamouse friends.
'Henry has no sense,' Julia was thinking. 'Skinny
Whiskers will eat him and I will never see him again.'

Twenty-four Balls of Soot

In the room far below, beside the door, Skinny Whiskers lay waiting. She knew that Henry Seamouse would never rest until he found his house. When he came through that door she was going to juggle him in her front paws for ages and ages. She purred with pleasure at the thought of it.

Skinny Whiskers heard a quiet PLOP behind her. Something had fallen down the chimney, something which looked like a tiny ball of soot.

PLOP. Another ball of soot appeared. Soon there were many balls of soot lying there, and some of them began to crawl towards the drum.

'That's funny,' thought Skinny Whiskers. 'I never knew that balls of soot could move.'

And then ... she noticed that some of those balls of soot had tails.

'That's very funny,' thought Skinny Whiskers. 'I never knew that balls of soot had tails!'

All of a sudden she realised the truth. "You're not soot!
You're Henry Seamouse and his seamouse friends!"
"Run for it!" shouted one of the balls of soot.
Twenty-four mice ran for their lives. There were so
many mice scooting across the carpet that Skinny
Whiskers didn't know which one to follow. One by one
they tumbled head-over-heels through the tiny hole at
the back of the drum, where the cat couldn't get at them
with her sharp claws.
They were filthy!
"ATCHOOO!" sneezed Mac, who had soot up his nose.
"Never mind," said Henry. "At least we're home again,
and that's the most important thing of all!"

19

A Noisy House

Anyone could see that the place was a mess.
All sorts of things had been broken in the moving and
all the hammocks were in a terrible twist. Henry's
furniture was upside-down and his lovely pictures were
crooked.

"Not to worry," he said. "Let's have something to eat and a long sleep, then we'll get the place ship-shape again." They ate some French cheese and some crispy bacon and lay down with their eyes closed. But they did not sleep for long.

TARA RA-BOOM! TARA RA-BOOM! THUMP WHACK!
TARA RA-BOOM! TARA RA-BOOM! THUMP WHACK!
It was the most amazing noise ever heard by a mouse.
Mac was so frightened that he fell out of his hammock!

"What's happening out there?" he squealed, covering up his large mouse ears. Through a small peep-hole, Henry Seamouse saw the problem. He saw Emily Robinson bashing the drum as hard as she could bash.

'This cannot go on,' thought Henry. 'No mouse could bear to live in such a noisy house. I'm going to have to think of something.'

He plugged up his ears and did some thinking. After a while he twirled his whiskers and began to smile ... he now knew exactly what he must do.

The Drum that could Hum

That night, when everyone was in bed, Emily Robinson crept downstairs for some trifle and cream.

'Yummy yummy,' she was thinking as she opened the fridge door. She wanted some trifle and she wanted it NOW.

Just as she lifted the dish she heard a strange noise coming from the living room.

Emily tip-toed in to see, but there was no-one there.
The drum lay on the floor in the moonlight, where she
had left it. But it was HUMMING!

'This is scary,' thought Emily. There wasn't another
sound in the whole house – only the drum humming
to itself ever so quietly.

'There must be a spook in it,' she thought, 'the kind that comes out on moonlit nights! I HATE spooks!' She shut her eyes in case she saw the awful thing and flew up the stairs.

"Mummy, Mummy, we've got a spook, we've got a spook," she cried. "Daddy, Daddy, there's a midnight spook in that rotten old drum."

"Don't be silly, dear," said Mr Robinson sleepily.

"A drum can't have a spook. There are no spooks."

"There are, and it's HUMMING. I don't want that drum any more and you'll have to get rid of it NOW."

Goodbye, Skinny Whiskers

In the morning, a van left Emily Robinson's house. There was a drum inside the van and there were twenty-four mice inside the drum. Henry Seamouse and his friends were on the move again.

When the van stopped some time later, there came a loud thump; then the van drove off, leaving the drum behind.

Everything was still and quiet. 'Perhaps too quiet,' thought Mac.

"Where are we?" he whispered. "We might be anywhere. Maybe this wasn't such a good idea."

"I shall go out and see," said Henry Seamouse.

One sniff at the door told him that there wasn't a cat around so out he went. All around him Henry saw high mountains and deep valleys made of rubbish and junk. They had come to a wonderfully smelly rubbish tip.

"Come out and see where we are," he shouted.

"It's a rubbish dump!"

29

One by one his seamouse friends followed him out.

"I smell cheese and onion crisps!"

"Yoghurt cartons! Mushy peas!"

"Oh boy!" they cried.

Mac put his nose in the air and it twitched when he breathed in the most lovely smell of all.

"We're near the sea," he said. "This is a seaside dump. Goodbye Skinny Whiskers and well done, Henry Seamouse."

Henry seemed well pleased by the way things had turned out for himself and his friends.

"I think we shall be happy here," he said.